BE KIND
BE SWEET

Be kind be sweet

Be nice to everyone you meet

Smile big give hugs

Give thanks to the Father above

And love goes around

And around and around

Love goes around and around

Say please say thanks

It's like putting money in the bank

Share things share love

Be ready to give whatever you've got

And love goes around

And around and around

Love goes around and around.

BE KIND
BE SWEET

be nice to
everyone
you
meet

a fun way to learn manners and counting

by
Tricia Lowenfield &
Mary Moore Lowenfield

Published by
Pumpkins Pansies Bunnies & Bears Press

Printed in the United States of America by Worzalla
First Edition 2008

Lowenfield, Tricia; Lowenfield Mary Moore
  Be Kind Be Sweet to Everyone You Meet/Lowenfield-1st Edition
  Summary: Through fun rhymes, colorful pictures, and Bible verses, kids learn
manners,counting and manners.
ISBN 978-0-9747367-1-6

Scripture taken from the Holy Bible, New International Version. Copyright 1973,1978,1984 International Bible Society. Used by permission of Zondervan Bible Publishers.

My deepest thanks to Nancy Scammacca who takes words and pictures and weaves them together to form the very book you are holding in your hands.

Pumpkins Pansies Bunnies & Bears Press
19 Treevine Ct.
The Woodlands, Texas 77381
281-785-0755
www.tricialowenfielddesign.com

To our family,
the back porch gang,
and the prayer group.

Tricia and Mary Moore

Please is a very nice thing to say,

count how many times

you can say it in a day!

Please is called the "magic word",
but who needs magic anyway? Just
be grateful for the nice things people
do for you everyday!

The good man brings good things out
of the good stored up in his heart.
For out of the overflow of his heart his mouth speaks.
Luke 6:45

two
kind words

Thank you is better than most anything,

When you say it to others

it will make their hearts sing!

You wouldn't believe how many
people forget to say
thank you!
It's only two words!

Be joyful always; pray continually,
give thanks in all circumstances.
1 Thessalonians 5:16-18

3
kind words

Give "I love you's" to people

it will be worthwhile-

Cause when they hear it from you

it will sure make them smile!

There are people in this world who
never hear the words "I Love You".
Isn't that sad?
Don't forget to tell the people you
love that you love them! In fact, tell
someone right now!

A new command I give you:
Love one another.
As I have loved you, so you must love one another.
By this all men will know that you are my disciples
if you love one another.
John 13:34-35

4 kind words

How do you do

Say "How do you do?" when you

meet someone new,

look in their eyes, shake their hands

and they will shake yours too!

It feels so good to be greeted
happily by old friends and new friends!
Make someone feel good!
Make a new friend!

I will not forget you!
See, I have engraved you on the palms of my hands.
Isaiah 49:16

So nice to meet you

5
kind
words

After you've met someone

and shook their hands,

say "It's so nice to meet you"

and that will be grand!

When you meet someone new, try to
think of a way to remember their name!
They will be so surprised that you remembered
their name when you see them again!

Let your conversation be always full of
grace, seasoned with salt,
so that you may know how to answer everyone.
Colossians 4:6

6 kind words

If someone walks by and their hands are full,

offer to open the door

just push or pull!

There have been many times when
you needed someone to help you open the door.
We all need help from one another sometimes!
So think of others, and help them out!

Here I am! I stand at the door and knock.
If anyone hears my voice and opens the door,
I will come in and eat with him, and he with me.
Revelations 3:20

7 kind words

If a friend looks busy,

with so much to do,

Say "Friend, Howdy do?

Can I help you?"

You want to know something funny
about helping?
When you give of yourself to others,
it makes you feel good too!

Two are better than one, because they have

a good return for their work:

If one falls down, his friend can help him up.

Ecclesiastes 4:9–10

8 kind words

When you make a little mess

at your home or as a guest,

Clean up after yourself

that will be the best.

Always be the first one to clean up!
Don't wait for someone to clean up after you.
If you can, make a game!
See who can clean up the fastest.

Jesus reached out his hand and touched the
man. "I am willing" he said.
"Be clean!" And immediately the leprosy left him.
Luke 5:13

9 kind words

When you sit down at a meal,

grab your napkin first, for real-

Put it in your lap,

and that will seal the deal!

Not everyone knows that it is very polite to put your napkin on your lap right when you sit down at the table. Some people even forget to put their napkin on their laps at all! Maybe if you do it, they will remember!

Dear children, let us not love with words or tongue but with actions and in truth.

1 John 3:18

Do not chew your food with your mouth open wide

10 kind words

Do not chew your food with your mouth

open wide,

It's best to keep it closed with the food all

inside!

Every meal is a good time to practice being polite. When chewing your food, keep it a secret!

So whether you eat or drink or
whatever you do,
do it all for the glory of God.
1 Corinthians 10:31

11

Give thanks always

in all that you do

You'll be surprised

at how glad it'll make you.

Here are some good times to
write thank you notes:
—when you receive gifts on your birthday or holidays
—when you go to someone's house for dinner
—when someone brings you ice cream when you are sick
—anytime

I have not stopped giving thanks for you,
remembering you in my prayers.
Ephesians 1:16

Pray at meals and at night. Always be kind. Please don't fight.

12 kind words

12

Praying is great

in fact it's the best

Down on your knees

at night before you rest.

Here is a great prayer to pray:
Dear Jesus,
Help me to be kind.
Help me to be sweet.
Help me to be nice to everyone I meet.
I love you. Thanks for loving me. Amen.

On my bed I remember you;
I think of you through the watches of the night.
Because you are my help,
I sing in the shadows of your wings.
Psalm 63:6–7

A Note to Adults

Dear Friends:

When my mother was of elementary age in the 1930's her public school in Dallas, Texas would daily recite these words which we know as the Lord's Prayer:

Our Father who art in Heaven hallowed (holy) be Thy name
Thy kingdom come, Thy will be done on earth as it is in Heaven.
Give us this day our daily bread and forgive us our trespasses
As we forgive those who trespass against us.
Lead us not into temptation and deliver us from evil
For thine is the Kingdom and the power and the glory.
Forever and ever.
Amen

Imagine that in the public schools of today! The public schools in those days inspired a kinder and sweeter time. You know as well as I do that not only is it not said today, but the kindnesses that it inspired have also been lost. I want you to know right away that I am guilty of not sharing the kindnesses this book illustrates. It is written as much for me as it is for any child who reads it or has it read to them.

But my husband insisted that our children not trespass on others because that is what being kind is. My children to this day are still reminding me to say please and thank you!! This whole little book is about thinking of others.

As these words are written today, the memory of last night comes to me. We were at the high school cafeteria for a tennis dinner and meeting with my youngest daughter. The meeting lasted lots longer than we had anticipated and we were anxious to leave. My daughter pointed out that a majority of parents and students had left their food and drink on the table and departed for the evening. She didn't think twice but started to clean up the mess. I on the other hand would not have thought about it. What a blessing to have as second nature the kindness to clean up for others so that someone else doesn't have to. It reminds me of a song that says, "think a little more of others and a little less of me."

Thinking about you,

Tricia

1 Please.

2 Thank you.

3 I love you.

4 How do you do?

5 So nice to meet you.

6 Open the door for a friend.

7 What can I do to help you?

8 Clean up after yourself when you make messes.

9 At the table put your napkin on your lap.

10 Do not chew your food with your mouth open wide.

11 Give thanks and write thank you notes when you receive gifts.

12 Pray at meals and at night. Always be kind. Please don't fight.

As for being KIND
and SWEET
let there be no end